Dear mouse friends,
Welcome to the world of

Geronimo Stilton

THE RODENT'S GAZETTE
EDITORIAL STAFF

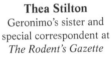

Geronimo Stilton
A learned and brainy
mouse; editor of
The Rodent's Gazette

Thea Stilton
Geronimo's sister and
special correspondent at
The Rodent's Gazette

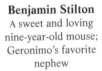

Trap Stilton
An awful joker;
Geronimo's cousin and
owner of the store
Cheap Junk for Less

Benjamin Stilton
A sweet and loving
nine-year-old mouse;
Geronimo's favorite
nephew

Geronimo Stilton

MOUSE VS WILD

Scholastic Inc.

Published by Scholastic Inc., *Publishers since 1920*, 557 Broadway, New York, NY 10012. SCHOLASTIC and associated logos are trademarks and/or registered trademarks of Scholastic Inc.

Stilton is the name of a famous English cheese. It is a registered trademark of the Stilton Cheesemakers' Association.

This book is a work of fiction. Names, characters, places, and incidents are either the product of the author's imagination or are used fictitiously, and any resemblance to actual persons, living or dead, business establishments, events, or locales is entirely coincidental.

ISBN 978-1-338-84802-1

Text by Geronimo Stilton
Original title *Il segreto di Porto Tanfoso*

Art Director: Iacopo Bruno
Cover art: Guiseppe Facciotto and Christian Aliprandi
Graphic Designer: Pietro Piscitelli/theWorldofDOT
Illustrations by Guiseppe Facciotto, Carolina Livio, Daria Cherchi, and Valeria Cairoli
Translated by Emily Clement
Special thanks to Anna Bloom
Interior design by Becky James

10 9 8 7 6 5 4 3 2 1   23 24 25 26 27

Printed in the U.S.A.   40
First printing 2023

FRIED LIKE A MOZZARELLA STICK

One windy late summer morning, I sat back and admired the leaves **swirling** outside my office window.

WHOOOSH

What a pleasant background for a **calm, peaceful** day of work!

Ah! But I haven't introduced myself. My name is Stilton, *Geronimo Stilton*, and I'm editor in chief of *The Rodent's Gazette*, the most **famouse** newspaper on Mouse Island!

In the newsroom, there's always lots to do — and I have my paws in every single thing! There are meetings to attend, photos to check, articles to write . . . It never ends!

Sometimes my whiskers *twitch* with all the STRESS!

That morning, however, I was feeling pretty **great**. I had my favorite **cheddar** smoothie to sip, and the sound of birds outside my window. The whole day **stretched** ahead of me — just me and my trusty old laptop!

But my **calm** moment did not last very long . . . **CRASH, SLAM!**

The door to my office suddenly **BURST** open.

"Hi, Geronimo!" shouted my cousin Trap. *Squeak!*

I was so surprised that I accidentally spilled my **SMOOTHIE** all over my desk. The breeze from Trap's entrance scattered my papers around, making

a **gigantic** mess.

Why did things like this always happen to me?!

I quickly tried to mop up the **MESS** with some nearby tissues. My snout wrinkled in **annoyance**.

"Why do you look like you're smelling moldy old cheese, Cousin?" Trap cried. "You seem **jumpy**. Did you sleep okay last night?"

"I slept just fine!" I muttered. "You need to learn to knock before you barge into a rodent's office!" I knelt down and reached under my desk to get the smoothie cup that had rolled away.

When I tried to stand back up . . .

BAM!

I smacked my head on the desk.

"**OWWW!** That hurt!!!" I yelled.

"See? You're **WObblier** than a slice of American cheese!" my cousin commented.

I went to sit back down at my desk, but the chair shifted and . . . **Boom!**

I fell to the floor, right on my tail!

"You're completely **OUT OF SORTS**!" Trap continued.

Then he came over and started muttering, "**PUFFY** eyes . . . **dull** fur . . . **slow** reflexes . . . Yes, yes, yes, I hate to say it,

Geronimo, but you look as tired as a three-day-old cheese sandwich that's been through the washing machine."

I sat up and wiggled my ears. "You don't know what you're talking about. I feel great. Well, I did until you showed up, anyway!"

"Geronimo, Geronimo, Geronimo." Trap shook his snout. "I know the look of a **STRESSED-OUT** mouse when I see one. You're fried like a mozzarella stick. But don't be a worryrat! I have just the solution for you!"

I sighed. Whatever Trap had up his **FURRY** sleeves was sure to stress me out even more!

VERY IMPORTANT MICE

Trap was eager to explain his grand idea to me. "Have you heard of the super-mega-resort **Mouse Luxe**?"

"No, I don't think so," I replied.

Trap gasped. "What?! Mouse Luxe is **famouse**! It is the most exclusive hotel on Mouse Island, and only true **VIMs**, Very Important Mice, can stay there! Their guest list is a who's who of the greatest **rodents** around!" He paused to take a deep breath before continuing, a grin stretching across his snout. "And now that guest list includes **you** — thanks to me!"

It took me a minute to grasp what he was saying. "**Me?** But I don't need a vacation!

And I can't leave the newspaper — I've got a lot of **cheese** on my plate right now."

"Don't get your tail in a twist, Geronimo. I've taken care of everything. And I had some **HELP** from Smoothie, obviously!"

"Smoothie?" I repeated, confused.

"Don't you remember my dear friend **Smoothie Slickpaws**?"

Holey Swiss cheese! Of course I remembered him . . . Thanks to him I'd taken one of the **WORST** vacations ever!*

* Read about it in my book *A Fabumouse Vacation for Geronimo.*

SMOOTHIE SLICKPAWS is the owner of the travel agency Trust Me You'll Like It. He wears sunglasses and sports a tan all year round (even in the winter when it's snowing!). He loves Hawaiian shirts, tacky souvenirs, and overcharging his customers!

I had hoped I would never have to hear his name ever again. I SHUDDERED. "Hmm. I appreciate the offer, Trap, but taking a vacation just isn't possible right now."

Trap didn't seem to have heard me. He pulled up the website for Mouse Luxe on his MousePad. "Look how **FABUMOUSE** it is! Wouldn't you like a nice, restful vacation here, all for free?"

I peered at the photos: sparkling seas, swaying palm trees, comfortable bungalows, multiple swimming pools . . . It did look nice. I could picture myself dipping my paws in a secluded HOT tub, sipping iced fondue, and reading that book on the history of cheese knives that I bought ages ago.

Trap sensed I was losing the will to RESIST. "A place like this is exactly what you need! Trust me."

I wasn't used to trusting Trap, that's for sure. My rodent sense was tingling. "Listen, this all looks **FABUMOUSE**, but just what does Smoothie Slickpaws have to do with it? And how can you afford to pay for all of this?"

"It would all be free!" Trap said. "There's just one thing —"

"I knew it!" I interrupted. "What's the catch?"

"Well, Smoothie's travel agency is sponsoring a **contest** that's open to all reporters in New Mouse City. The PRIZE is a vacation at the resort for them and a guest. The reporter will get EXCLUSIVE access behind the scenes and the ability to interview all the hotel's **important** guests."

Suddenly, it all made sense. "You want me to WIN this vacation so I can take you to the resort with me!"

Trap squeaked and threw his paws in the air. "**Exactly!** After all, without me, you wouldn't even know about this contest. And I can definitely help you win. But it's not just about me — think of what a **golden** opportunity this is! Imagine how many selfies I could take with the VIMs staying there . . . umm . . . I mean, just think how many **scoops** you could get for *The*

Rodent's Gazette! Exclusive interviews . . . **FABUMOUSE** photos . . ."

That did sound **COMPELLING**, but I was still a little uncertain. "What does this **contest** involve, exactly?"

"Oh, practically nothing, Geronimo! You'll see!" Trap replied.

I **groaned**. That didn't sound good!

"No **risk**, no reward! The **early** mouse gets the **luxury** vacation!" Trap cried, and charged out of my office, waving his paw for me to follow.

SQUEAK!

GERONIMO
THE GREAT!

Trap pushed me into a waiting taxi. "To the New Mouse City **heliport**, and step on it!" he squeaked, sliding in next to me.

Whaaaaat? What did a heliport have to do with winning a resort vacation?

A few minutes later, we reached our destination. Trap JuMPED out of the taxi, and I rushed to join him.

"Hurry, Smoothie is waiting for you!" he told me, waving me forward.

I looked to where he was pointing a paw. A helicopter sat waiting for rodents to board.

All my **FUR** stood on end. "That's for me?" I *squeaked*, confused.

Trap nodded. "This is where the contest

kicks off," he explained. But before he could say more, Smoothie Slickpaws had appeared.

"Good to see you!" Smoothie said. "Welcome to my contest!" He gave Trap a **BIG** hug. Then he lowered his **SUNGLASSES** and looked me over from the end of my nose to the tip of my tail. "Here you are, Geronimo the Great! Still the same old stinky cheese, eh?"

I twisted my tail in my paws. "Geronimo, it's just Geronimo!"

"Okay, you got it, Geronimo!" Smoothie chuckled, making my whiskers twitch.

It was then that I realized we weren't alone on the helipad.

It looked like the other contestants had already arrived. I glanced over at them and gasped. There among the crowd was none other than Sally Ratmousen, the editor in chief of *The Daily Rat*!

Great globs of greasy cat guts. She was my greatest **NEMESIS**!

As soon as she saw me, my rival let out a squeal. "I thought I smelled old cheese. Look who it is, the editor in chief of the most boring and useless newspaper in New Mouse City!"

My fur BRISTLED. "Hello, Sally. How are you?" I asked through **GRITTED** teeth.

She sighed. "You might as well quit the competition before it starts, Stilton. I'd hate to see you embarrass yourself. Gal Gouda and I are going to

Sally Ratmousen

Gal Gouda

win this whole thing, so there's really no need for you to put yourself through all this." The two of them smirked at me.

"Nice to meet you, Geronimo," Gal said, holding out her paw.

I had heard of Gal before. She wrote a column called "Fabumouse Fashion!" in Sally's newspaper. Gal had always seemed kinder and friendlier than Sally, but now it was clear they were a united front. I plastered a polite smile on my snout, and we shook paws. 🐾

I saw Gal roll her eyes toward Sally, who laughed. We stepped away from them, and I glanced around us.

There was one other reporter in the contest: the famouse RUGBY champion Paula Pecorino, who hosted a sports show on MouseTV.

"Stilton!" Paula greeted me, coming over. "Good to see you! I didn't know you were entering this contest." She SQUEEZED my paw with a very firm grip.

Next to her stood an elegant rodent. "Esteemed Mr. Stilton, I am his eminence the Count Rattington von Cheese Curd, boyfriend of the sweet lady next to me. I am very pleased to make your acquaintance!"

"Sweet lady"? Was he talking about Paula? I had never heard her described that way before. But I guess every CHEESE SLICE has their cracker.

Our conversation was interrupted by Smoothie. "The moment has arrived to climb on board this

Rattington von Cheese Curd

Paula Pecorino

GEM," he said, pointing to the helicopter.

I started to tremble like a cheese soufflé. As you know, my dear rodent friends, I'm not always the BRAVEST mouse around. And if there's one thing that turns me into a scaredy-mouse more than anything else, it's flying!

"We all have to get on board that thing?" I squeaked.

"What did you think, Stilton, that we were just going to flap our paws and fly away?" Sally teased.

"B-but I — I don't tr-trust . . ." I stuttered, turning as PALE as mozzarella.

"Don't get cold paws now, Geronimo!" Smoothie cried. "You'll see, a little altitude will do you good!"

The pilot started the helicopter's engine and the blades began to spin quickly.

FLAP FLAP FLAP FLAP

"Jump on board, contestants!" Smoothie cried. "A true **ADVENTURE** awaits you!"

SIGH. I guess I was doing this!!

WIN OR SQUEAK!

The helicopter rose into the air. I clutched my stomach and tried not to look down.

I wanted to go right back to my desk and my CHEDDAR smoothie.

The other contestants seemed much more excited than I was.

"Look, Happy Hills!" cried Gal Gouda, pointing out her window. Everymouse followed her paw to look out the window. Everymouse but me, that is. Twisty cheese sticks! My snout was spinning!

"Cousin, open your eyes and look at our

island! Isn't it **amazing**?" Trap said to me.

"Sure, Trap, it's **great**," I said, opening one eye and then quickly shutting it again. "But just where are we going?"

Trap started to answer, but Smoothie clapped his paws together. "Attention, all mice! It's time to officially begin my **FABUMOUSE** contest! I'm calling it Win or Squeak!

"In order to win a week at the **Mouse Luxe** resort, you contestants must spend three days in a super-exclusive area. There you will undergo **FOUR CHALLENGES**! But be warned: there are absolutely no cell phones allowed, and no contacting the outside world!"

My whiskers **trembled**. What kind of contest was this? I should never have trusted Trap!

Some of the other rodents started to look concerned. "Where is it you're taking us again?" Sally asked.

"Don't be a worryrat, madame! We're traveling to none other than . . . Port Stinky!!!" Smoothie said.

Squeak!!! Port Stinky?!

"But that's the wildest, most isolated, and . . . stinkiest place on Mouse Island!" I cried.

"You know, it's funny," Smoothie said thoughtfully, stroking his whiskers. "None of my clients have ever wanted to go to Port Stinky before. Even though I have EXCLUSIVE access to it!"

Sally squealed. "Are you joking?! Port Stinky is famouse for its terrible smell!"

Count Rattington wrinkled his snout. "I am extraordinarily sensitive to odors."

Paula gave him a friendly pat on the shoulder. "Maybe it won't be that bad," she said hopefully.

"You were saying something about four challenges," Sally said. "Just what are those going to be?"

But before Smoothie could reply, Gal Gouda cried, "Look, we're almost at Port Stinky!"

I screwed up my courage and snuck a look out the window. In the distance, I could see the Port Stinky lighthouse.

Aside from that, there wasn't a lot to see. There had once been a huge factory here that had polluted the entire area, filling the water with waste and making the air smell terrible.

The inhabitants had all moved away and Port Stinky and its beaches were now totally abandoned.

We were about to be the first rodents in a very long time to step a paw into this area!

JUMPING INTO THE CONTEST!

The helicopter started to descend. I looked out the window, but all I could see below us was water, water, and more water . . . We were still dozens of feet away from the Port Stinky lighthouse, with the pier and ruins of the old factory beyond it.

"Are we landing on the beach?" I asked Smoothie.

He WINKED at me. "Landing? Who said anything about landing?"

Smoothie rolled up the sleeves of his Hawaiian shirt. "The first challenge is about to begin! It consists of . . . a jump into the sea from fifteen feet up! Then you will swim to shore. You must complete this first stage in order to continue on and be in contention for the **TOP** prize."

All my fur stood on end. My whiskers began to twitch. There was only one thing worse than riding in a helicopter — and that was **jumping** out of one! Squeak! I felt dizzy with fear. Then . . .

BAAAAAAAAM!

I fainted.

Trap waved smoked **mozzarella** under my nose to revive me. (Why are his pockets always full of cheese?!)

Geronimo?

"Geronimo?" Trap called. "Are you **okay**? The **jumping** is about to start."

I sat up **slowly**, my head in my paws. "No, no, no! I'm not **jumping**, and that's my final word!" I protested.

Trap had already put on the **gear** for the jump. "I know you can do it. Look, I'll go first and show you that there's nothing to be afraid of." Then he positioned himself at the helicopter's door. "Hey, folks, check out the **DIVE** of a champion!" He stepped out, and I let out a **squeal**.

Two seconds later, I heard a

SPLAAAAAAASH!

Trap had dropped into the water, making a huge **splash**.

Smoothie let out a little cough, took out a notepad, and scrawled something down. "He certainly has **COURAGE** . . . technique, not so much. Not exactly an amazing dive. I give it a . . . FIVE."

Then Smoothie looked up and pointed his pen at Gal. "Okay, Gal — you're up next!"

One by one, all the other rodents put on their gear and launched themselves tail first into the **SEA** below.

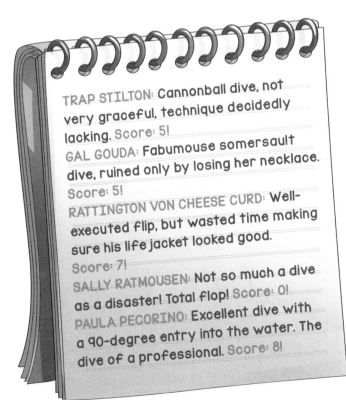

TRAP STILTON: Cannonball dive, not very graceful, technique decidedly lacking. Score: 5!

GAL GOUDA: Fabumouse somersault dive, ruined only by losing her necklace. Score: 5!

RATTINGTON VON CHEESE CURD: Well-executed flip, but wasted time making sure his life jacket looked good. Score: 7!

SALLY RATMOUSEN: Not so much a dive as a disaster! Total flop! Score: 0!

PAULA PECORINO: Excellent dive with a 90-degree entry into the water. The dive of a professional. Score: 8!

How scary!

Eep! Now I was the only one left!

I put on my life jacket and inched my way to the helicopter door. I peered at the ocean below me, trembling from the tops of my ears to the tip of my tail.

My head spun like a ball of mozzarella in a clothes dryer. I didn't want to do this! No vacation was worth all of this trouble.

I was about to sit back down, but a GUST of wind shook the helicopter and I TUMBLED right out into the air!

"Helllpppp!!!" I screamed, squeezing my eyes shut.

SPLASH! **GLUB!** **SPUTTER!** **BLUB!**

I hit the water with a **SPLASH**.

I swam my way up through the water and burst through the surface, spitting out **seawater** and gasping for air.

My life jacket kept me **bobbing** in the waves as I looked around for the beach. I still had to **swim** all the way to dry land! It looked so far away . . . I kicked my paws and began to swim as hard as I could.

When I finally made it to the **beach**, everymouse sat drying off in the sun. Smoothie's helicopter had landed, and he rushed to help me out of the **WAVES**.

"We have a winner!" he cried, raising my paw in his. "The best dive belonged to the great Geronimo Stilton!"

Whaaaat? I was too shocked to respond.

"You were **INCREDIMOUSE**! You did a reverse dive with a triple flip and a ninety-degree entry into the water!"

I just stared at him.

"I scored it a perfect **ten**! The first win of the contest goes to Team Geronimo and Trap!"

How to Build a Hut

Paula gave me a **huge** hug. "Good job, Stilton! Great dive!"

Smoothie handed out DRY clothes to everymouse. He gave me a WHITE jersey that was too tight, green pants that were too long, and a STRAW HAT that was too big.

Sally Ratmousen pushed her way to the front, looking **angry**. "I would like a recount before we go on! I can't believe that you would score this cheese curd for brains higher than me!" She waved a paw in my direction.

Smoothie shook his head. "Absolutely not. We must move on!" He **clapped** his paws together and motioned for all of us to gather

around him. "This will be your home for the next three days."

We were all silent for a minute. Litter lined the beach and bobbed in the waves. Beyond the beach grew a thorny, tangled forest. Past that loomed a severe-looking **MOUNTAIN**. A ~~**BAD**~~ smell wafted around us. Port Stinky was living up to its name already.

"Well, it certainly is **peaceful**. Sort of," added Gal Gouda, frowning.

"Just where are we supposed to sleep?" Sally asked through GRITTED teeth.

Smoothie smirked. "The **SECOND CHALLENGE** is to build your own hut!"

"But what if we don't know how to do that?" I asked.

"Don't be a worryrat, Geronimo! I believe in you — in all of you! That's what this contest is all about — testing your resourcefulness, bravery, and **strength**. I know you all have it in you."

I definitely didn't have anything in me other than the lemon ricotta pancakes I had eaten for breakfast!

"It's time for the **SECOND CHALLENGE** to officially begin!" Smoothie continued. "I'd work **FAST** if I were you. The evenings can get pretty **chilly** around here!"

I groaned and turned to face Trap. "*Why, why, why* did I let you talk me into doing this contest?!" I cried.

Trap put his paws on my shoulders. "**Relax**, Geronimo! Don't you know that I'm practically a professional **HUT** builder?"

Then he headed for the **forest**. "Come on, help me gather some supplies. You look for **branches**. I'm going to gather some strong **vines**."

I followed him into the forest. I had to be careful not to get scratched, tripped, or smacked by any **TREE** limbs!

After a while, I was **sweaty**, but pretty pleased with the armload of branches I'd managed to collect. I made my way back down to the beach and fell onto the sand next to Trap.

"It's time to start the real work!" Trap cried.

After a few hours, our hut was complete . . . more or less.

"Are you sure it'll stay up?" I **whispered**.

"Of course! Trust me!" Trap said.

He patted the wall of our hut and . . . *baaaang!*

In the **twitch** of a whisker, it had completely collapsed!

Squeak, what a disaster!

Paula and Rattington were doing better. Their hut looked a little **UNSTABLE**, but at least it was still standing. Sally and Gal had done a fabumouse job. Their **HUT** looked as solid as the mountain that loomed behind us.

Toasted cheese sandwiches, how had they done it?!

Smoothie had no doubt about the winner of the second challenge. "**Congratulations**, Sally and Gal, for your incredimouse work!"

Sally **cheered** and pumped her paw in the air.

But she wasn't **cheering** for long. Now that the second challenge was complete, it was time for us to spend the night on the beach.

Oh nooo!

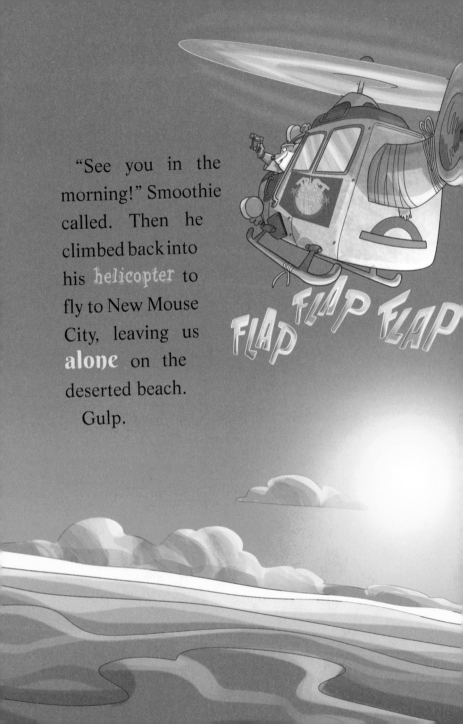

"See you in the morning!" Smoothie called. Then he climbed back into his helicopter to fly to New Mouse City, leaving us **alone** on the deserted beach.

Gulp.

FLAP FLAP FLAP

GERONIMO AFTER DARK

The sun was **setting** as Trap and I, with the help of Paula and Rattington, finished rebuilding our hut.

And then my stomach started to GROWL with hunger!

Luckily, each contestant had been given:

- ➊ A sleeping bag (*full of holes*)
- ➋ A canteen of water (*warm*)
- ➌ A piece of cheese (*moldy*)
- ➍ A flashlight (*on low battery*)

It quickly became dark, so **DARK** that you couldn't tell a piece of provolone from a piece of cheddar.

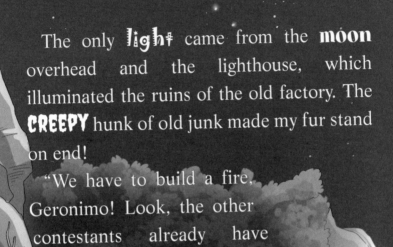

The only **light** came from the **moon** overhead and the lighthouse, which illuminated the ruins of the old factory. The **CREEPY** hunk of old junk made my fur stand on end!

"We have to build a fire, Geronimo! Look, the other contestants already have theirs going," Trap said.

"But we have a **FLASHLIGHT!**" I said.

Trap **rolled** his eyes. "Don't be a silly old cheese. We need a **FIRE** for warmth. And to scare away the **wild** beasts."

Squeak! **WILD BEASTS?!** Blistering balls of mozzarella!

Trap noticed that my snout had gone as white as a bowl of **ricotta**, and he

patted me on the back. "Don't be a scaredy-mouse, Geronimo! A while ago, I worked as a tour guide with an **ADVENTURE** company. I know all about this stuff. The first thing is for you to go back into the forest and gather some wood for us."

"Me?" I squeaked. "It's so dark, I can't see my paw in front of my face. And you just said that there could be wild beasts in there, just waiting for a **tasty** mouse treat!"

Trap chuckled. "Shake your tail and get us some fuel — the sooner we get this **FIRE** roaring, the better!"

Trembling like cottage cheese, I grabbed the **wonky** flashlight and returned to the forest.

Squeeeeak!!!

Quick as a **flash**, I grabbed the first branches I could find on the ground and took them back to Trap, who lit a fire (after many, many tries).

Finally, it was time to go to sleep. I slipped into my **sleeping bag** and tried to relax. But the breeze was **cold**, and my mind raced with thoughts of what creatures could be lurking at the forest's edge.

I couldn't wait for the **sun** to rise!

A Lovely Bunch of Coconuts!

That night, I slept very little. It was very cold, very SCARY, and, just like Port Stinky's name implied, very smelly!

I had just drifted off when a thunDerous noise jolted me awake.

FLAP FLAP FLAP FLAP

I stuck my nose out of the hut and saw that the thing making all that racket was Smoothie Slickpaws's helicopter.

"RiSe and shine, rodents!" he shouted, climbing down the ladder. "It's time for the THIRD CHALLENGE."

"Wait, what about breakfast?!" I asked. My stomach RUMBLED.

"Breakfast with what? We only have a **moldy** piece of cheese," Trap complained.

"I'm happy to hear you mention food," Smoothie said.

I lifted my snout hopefully and looked around to see if buffet tables had somehow **magically** appeared. Was Smoothie going to offer us a hearty meal before we continued the competition? Maybe his helicopter was full of cheese buns, mozzarella fritters, and **fontina smoothies**.

"Because the third challenge consists of coming up with your own **INCREDIMOUSE** meal . . . using only things you can find around you!"

Paula let out a **squeak**. "But the only edible things here are **COCONUTS** . . . Pollution has killed most of the other kinds of plants!"

Smoothie nodded. "Excellent observation, Paula! A stroke of **luck**, right? Where else could you find such fabumouse coconuts?!" He looked thoughtful. "New challenge! Today, the rodent who *gathers* the most coconuts will win the third challenge."

Was he serious? All of us exchanged *confused* looks.

But apparently he was serious.

"Ready, set, go!" Smoothie yelled.

The other contestants scattered into the *forest*. The coconuts were located at the tops of the palm trees . . . so high up, they were practically unreachable!

"Easy peasy, *lemon* squeezey," Sally declared smugly. She started to *shake* the nearest palm tree.

❶ After a moment a coconut fell . . . right onto my paw! *Ow!* That hurt!

"Come on, Geronimo, let's do that, too!" Trap urged me.

2 I tried to climb up a trunk, but just when I had almost reached a coconut, I **slipped** all the way to the ground, landing right on my tail. *Owww!*

Trap **shook** his snout. "Leave it to me, **Cousin**!" he said.

He took a long branch and started to shake the leaves . . . until a coconut **3** **FELL** on my other paw! *Owww!*

The competition wasn't

going well for Trap and me, but Sally and Gal hadn't gathered **anything** yet, either.

As for Rattington, he stood staring up at the trees. "Me, climb up there? I don't think so! If my mother, the fabumousely elegant Countess De Licatis, ever **heard** about this, she would die of **shame!**"

He and Paula hadn't gathered a single coconut so far. Just then a **GRIN** spread across Paula's snout. "I have

an **amazing** idea! Hand me a coconut! It's really not so different from a RUGBY ball."

With that, she placed it on the sand, focused for a moment, and then gave it a powerful KICK.

The coconut FLEW through the air, hit a palm tree branch, and . . .

THUNK!

A huge bunch of coconuts fell to the ground!

Soon, Paula had gathered up a mountain of coconuts nearly as tall as her.

Smoothie clapped his paws together in delight. "That's what I like to see! There's no question in my mind, mice — the winner of the third challenge is Paula and Rattington!"

Relax, Geronimo!

The rugby champion was a true sportswoman and Rattington a true gentlemouse, so they offered to share their **MOUNTAIN** of coconuts with everyone for breakfast.

"Thank you!" I squeaked, taking one.

Sally snatched up a pile for herself, muttering, "I had the same idea, I just hadn't had a chance to try it yet!"

As we munched on our coconuts, Smoothie updated us on where the competition stood. "Mice, here are the standings: one point for Geronimo and Trap, one point for Sally and Gal, and one point for Paula and Rattington. **You're all tied!**"

Sally shot me an icy stare. "Don't get too excited about the prize, Stilton. I'm going to **WIN**, I promise you!"

Then she turned to Smoothie. "Go on, what's the next challenge?"

"That's it for today, actually," Smoothie replied. "We'll resume the competition **tomorrow**. You can enjoy a little **relaxation** time on this **beautiful** beach!"

We all exchanged glances. This place was many things — garbage covered, **smelly**, cold — but beautiful, it was not!

Rattington sneered in **disgust**. "But this place is a **trash** heap!" He put his snout in his paws. "Just when you think you've gotten used to the **STENCH**, it seems to get stronger! I need to lie down," he moaned, wandering away.

Trap was the only rodent who didn't seem bothered by the prospect of another **long** day at Port Stinky. "Hey, Gal," he called, "want to take a STROLL on the beach with me?"

Sally waved her paws and shook her snout. "Absolutely not. Gal and I need to plot — I mean, sunbathe. **Alone!**" Sally stomped off down the beach, pulling Gal along with her.

Trap shrugged and started a game of rugby with Paula.

What I really needed was a **nap**! I chose a SUNNY spot on the sand, and cleared away the biggest pieces of trash. Then I coated myself in sunscreen and lay down for a little rest. Just what I needed. I tried not to focus on the **smell**; instead I listened to the WAVES and pretended I was far, far away . . . Soon I had fallen fast **asleep**.

WILD BEASTS!

I had been asleep for a little while when a **LOW** noise woke me up with a start.

GRRRR . . .

I opened one eye . . .

GRRRRROOO . . .

Then the other one

GRRRRROOOAAARRR!

Twisted cat tails! Had wild beasts finally come to eat us?!

"Help!" I squealed in terror. I jumped to my paws and ran for the water.

Without thinking twice, I leaped into the sea and started swimming away quickly. When it seemed like I was a good distance from shore, I paused, bobbing in the water. Panting, I turned to look back toward the beach. At first I didn't see anyone. Had they all been eaten?

But then I spotted Trap, laughing and waving.

"You're a real scaredy-mouse! Those noises were just me pretending to be a wild beast!" He laughed again.

I wrinkled my snout, annoyed. Now I was all wet for no good reason. With a sigh, I swam back to shore.

"Not funny," I grumbled, sitting on my towel.

Helllppp!

I lay down again. Little by little, the SUN dried my fur. The waves sang me a lullaby. My eyes closed, and then . . .

SPLASH!

A bucketful of cold water flooded over me, soaking me from the ends of my whiskers to the tip of my tail.

"It's icy cold!" I complained. "Why would you do that?!"

Trap, the bucket still in his paws, looked sheepish. "I was worried you were going to get heatstroke, baking in the sun like that."

"Enough with the water!" I yelled, moving my towel a little farther away.

I checked around me to make sure Trap was gone, lay down, relaxed, and fell asleep again.

I had a fabumouse dream where I swam through a sea of cheese fondue. It was so dense that I could barely move my paws . . . In fact, I couldn't move them at all!

I woke up. I still couldn't move my legs. "Help!" I shouted.

Someone had built a huge sandcastle on

top of me, pinning my paws to the ground!

A crab scuttled over me and PINCHED my snout.

"Hey, get out of here," I squeaked. It let go and SCURRIED off over the sand.

Trap appeared next to me and **giggled**. "Paula and I had a sand sculpture contest!"

"GET ME OUT OF HERE!" I squealed.

Trap helped dig me out. We spent the rest of the day making repairs to our hut. By the time evening fell, I was ready to eat my share of the COCONUTS for dinner and go right to sleep. The sooner we could put this day behind us, the better!

I had only just fallen **asleep** when I was awakened by a CREAKING sound outside the hut. Squeak!

Then the sound of footsteps. Squeak! Squeak!

Then a **SHADOW** blocked the moonlight. *Squeak! Squeak! Squeak!*

I whispered to Trap, who was **snoring** in the sleeping bag next to mine, "Psst! Wake up! Wake up!

But my cousin couldn't hear me over his own **snoring**.

Quick as a *FLASH* I got out of my sleeping bag to peer outside.

There really was something outside, but it didn't seem to be a beast. Maybe . . . it was one of the other contestants?

Who's there?!

I found the courage to **whisper**, "Who's there?"

"It's just me, Gal."

A few moments later, I saw her: it really was Gal, walking toward her **HUT**. What a relief! I let out a *SIGH*.

But what was she doing taking a walk at this time of **night**?

As if she'd read my mind, she **whispered**, "Every night I go for a stroll. I like to stretch my paws when no one else is around."

I waved and then, feeling **calmer**, went back into my hut to fall asleep. Gal was an awfully **nice rodent** . . . What a shame she was working with Sally Ratmousen!

THE FINAL
CHALLENGE

The next morning I awoke to Sally shouting as she ran up and down the beach, "I want to go H0ME! I want to go H0ME!!!!"

Gal tried to calm her down. "It's the last day, Sally. Soon we will be enjoying a **FABUMOUSE** time at the Mouse Luxe resort."

I wanted to go home, too! I couldn't bear to eat another piece of **COCONUT**!

At last, Smoothie's helicopter could be heard in the distance. Before long, it was touching down on the beach. He emerged from inside, a **wide** grin on his snout.

"It's time for the **FINAL CHALLENGE**!" he cried. "The team with the most points after this will win a free vacation at the Mouse Luxe resort!"

My whiskers **trembled**. Every task so far had been HORRIBLE. Just what did Smoothie have up his sleeve now?

We all stood silently, listening closely as Smoothie continued. "The final challenge will be *orienteering*!"

We all stared at him blankly, waiting for an explanation. "I will give you a map to follow, and each team must make their way as quickly as they can to the finish. Prepare to get in touch with nature as you explore Port Stinky!"

I turned as PALE as mozzarella. That must mean we had to go back into the forest . . . where the wild beasts lived. Squeak! I did not want to become a mouse meatball!

Smoothie gave each pair of us an envelope. "In these envelopes you'll find your MAP of the island and directions to reach the first destination."

Sally opened her envelope immediately. She squealed. "But there's just numbers and letters here! Is this a joke?"

"Ah, it's no joke," Smoothie replied. "That's the fun of orienteering! The number

It's the final challenge!

and the letter refer to one of the quadrants on the MAP. That's where you'll find the first FLAG."

"The first flag?" I asked. My head felt like scrambled eggs and cheese.

Smoothie nodded. "Each team must find their first FLAG. Once there, you will also find the clue that tells you where to locate the second flag. Every team has their own set of flags to locate. The team that finds both of their flags and brings them here first will WIN the competition!"

Rattington sighed. "This seems like a lot of effort for a free vacation."

Paula elbowed him playfully. "Come on, **TEAMMATE**! We've come this far. We can do it!"

"That's the spirit!" Smoothie cheered. "And what's more, you'll have a **COMPASS** to use!" he said, handing one to each pair.

Then he raised his paws in the air. "Ready? Let the final challenge of the competition begin!"

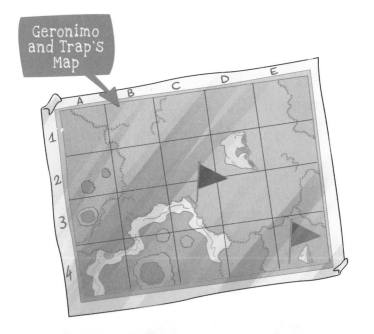

Geronimo and Trap's Map

I NEED A CAT NAP!

Sally and Gal took off at *FULL SPEED* toward the forest without even consulting their map. **Odd**. They must have been feeling confident. Maybe Gal's **nighttime** walks had given her some sort of information about the area? But I didn't have time to waste wondering. Trap and I had to figure out where we were *GOING*!

Hurry, let's go!

Trap read our destination off of the map: "E4!"

"Squeak! It's in the middle of the f-f-forest! O-over th-there," I stammered.

I looked up as Paula and Rattington sprinted past us into the DARK and gloomy woods.

"Let's go, Cousin!" Trap cried. He CHARGED away toward the forest, too.

Reluctantly, I followed. Under the cover of trees, the air was cool and HEAVY. I kept my eyes glued to the ground so I wouldn't trip over any roots ... or step on any wild beasts. SHUDDER!

Let's go!

I was too worked up to pay much attention to our path.

We had been WALKING for some time when Trap stopped short. I BOUNCED into him like a mozzarella ball falling to the ground.

"Geronimo, are you sure we're going the right way?" Trap asked, looking around.

"Um, I'm not sure." I glanced down at the map. Several paths had been marked out for us, but we didn't appear to be on a real trail anymore. Everywhere I looked, all I saw was wild plants and ROCKS. The only thing I recognized was Port Stinky's signature smell!

"Let's walk a little farther and see if we come across a trail," I suggested. We didn't have much choice.

Eventually we found ourselves in front of

a **huge** boulder shaped like a **dolphin**.

"Wait, I saw this on the map!" I cheered.

But then I realized that this boulder was located in quadrant D2 — nowhere near where we were supposed to be.

I pulled my whiskers in frustration. "We went the wrong way! What a disaster! We have to figure out the right way to go, or we'll never even get to the first flag!"

I pulled the compass out of my pocket and

reoriented the map. "Let's try this way!" I said, and we set off through the forest.

Along the way:

1 I tripped four times on roots and fell down. *(Ow!)*

2 I ended up in two enormouse muddy **puddles**. *(Yuck! So stinky!)*

3 I was hit thirteen times in the nose by branches that Trap had pulled back to open up a path through the forest. *(Youch!)*

Youch!

But finally, I caught sight of a rock formation shaped like slices of **cheese**. We had reached area E4!

"Our flag is down there!" Trap cried.

We *RACED* down a **STEEP** hill to grab it. Just as Smoothie had said, there was a second set of coordinates tied to the FLAG.

"Let's take a look . . ." Trap said. "It says our second flag is located in zone C3!"

I looked at the map. "Oh no! That's far northwest of where we are now, near a stream." I **groaned**. "We're never going to win!"

SUPER STINK ATTACK!

We tried to walk quickly, but it was hard work in the **DENSE** forest. And we still weren't sure we were going in the right direction.

"Geronimo, I think we've seen that tree before," Trap said.

"Maybe, I don't know, hmm . . ." I replied, turning the map around in my paws.

Suddenly, Trap grabbed my arm. "Look over there!" he cried.

Look over there!

Silly string cheese, what had he seen? **A wild beast?!**

Trembling like cottage cheese, I looked to see what Trap was pointing at and . . .

burst out **laughing**. A small, **fuzzy** animal rooted through the underbrush.

"Trap, don't be a scaredy-mouse. That's just some kind of squirrel, or maybe a raccoon," I said.

Trap shook his snout. "**Skunk!**" he shouted. "**Skunk!!!**"

The **CREATURE** turned its head in our direction and let out a long, low **HISSSS**.

I gulped. "Uh, Trap, let's just —"

But then it turned and raised its tail in our direction.

"**RUN!**" Trap squealed.

But it was too late! From beneath its tail a cloud of stench erupted . . .

SWIIIIIISSSSSHHHH!

Trap **dragged** me by the arm as we tried to escape the disgusting smell — which was much, much, much worse than the regular air in Port Stinky!

With each step, I looked back to check if the **SKUNK** was following us. Fortunately, it wasn't. After a while, I was out of breath, and panting.

"Trap . . . maybe now we can . . . stop . . ." I huffed.

Trap slowed down but didn't stop. He

SQUEEZED himself through a curtain of thin trees and waved for me to follow him.

As I stepped through the trees, I could see we were in a small clearing. I took deep breaths in and out, trying to catch my breath. I felt like a triple-fried mozzarella ball!

"Trap, do you notice anything different about this part of the forest?" I asked. I took another deep gulp of air.

My cousin sniffed the BREEZE. "Geronimo! It's a little less stinky here!"

I nodded. "And this is a nice leafy TREE . . ." I said, pointing to the tree in the middle of the clearing.

"And green, healthy grass," Trap noted, surprised.

"And even some flowers!" I pointed my paw at a few clusters of blooms with bees buzzing around them.

How was it possible that in this **GROSS**, polluted, abandoned area, a green corner was hiding? I checked my MAP.

"This must be the Desert Clearing. But it's not a **desert** at all!" I said. "Maybe Port Stinky isn't as completely hopeless as everyone thinks!"

Trap looked thoughtful. "Speaking of hopeless things . . . How far are we from the second flag?"

But I let out a gasp. "Trap, look over there!"

A FABUMOUSE DISCOVERY!

At the foot of the central tree grew a flower I'd only ever seen in books and online. It had a very thin stem and delicate white petals in a strange shape.

I was certain. This had to be a rare GHOST orchid, a fragile and ENDANGERED flower!

My sister, Thea, special correspondent of *The Rodent's Gazette*, had photographed

THE GHOST ORCHID grows in places with a warm and humid climate. Its stem is so thin that the flower seems to be almost suspended in the air, just like a ghost.

some specimens on one of her dangermouse **trips** around the world.

Somehow, in a clearing in the HEART of Port Stinky . . . a plant as rare and precious as the ghost orchid had managed to survive!

What a **FABUMOUSE** discovery! I was jumping out of my **FUR** with excitement.

From behind me, Trap coughed to get my attention. "That's a very pretty flower, Geronimo, but we should shake our tails and get going. We must be close to the second flag after all that running."

"Forget the second flag. We must go back to the beach right away! This orchid means there's hope for Port Stinky — that's enormmouse news!!"

"Whaaat? Do you have **cheddar** for brains, Cousin? We can't go back without our flag!"

I shook my snout. "This is bigger than some silly competition. Look at it!"

What a discovery!

Trap frowned and rubbed his snout. "It's just a *flower* that looks like a blob of melted cheese."

"Listen, Trap. That's not just any flower! It's an extremely RARE flower: we must get back to New Mouse City to tell everyone about this **FABUMOUSE** discovery!"

"Geronimo, be serious for one minute. We're a whisker away from taking home the grand prize. We can't give up! Think of being on the beach at the Mouse Luxe resort: the crystal-clear sea, the palm trees, the SUN, the unlimited cheese smoothies. First we win this vacation, then we tell everyone about your discovery, what do you say?"

I shook my snout, determined not to give in. "No, no, no! We can't wait . . . The true prize isn't what you find at a VIM resort,

Trap. It's discovering that nature is healing — finally, after all these years!"

Trap crossed his paws, a **frown** on his snout. Squeak! What if we couldn't agree on what to do next?!

SOMETHING'S NOT RIGHT . . .

At last, Trap agreed to follow me back to the **beach**, giving up his dream of winning a free luxury vacation. "Okay, let's do it. But only because I happen to be one of the world's greatest plant lovers. Did you know I once won a trophy for my gardening skills?"

I rolled my eyes but let Trap tell me a long, boring story about his prizewinning tomato plants on the walk back to the beach.

Finally, we reached the pier at Port Stinky, right in front of the lighthouse.

Smoothie sat on a lounge chair. He was

drinking a frozen ricotta shake and taking in the last of the day's SUNSHINE while music played loudly from his portable radio.

When he saw us, he turned off the **RADIO**. "Here you are!" he called.

"I have an ANNOUNCEMENT to make!" I cried.

But then Sally appeared, squealing, "The only important announcement left to make now is that I am the **winner** of this competition!!!"

I am the winner!

She waved both her team's flags high in the air.

I squeaked, "Congratulations. But I need to announce something much more important . . ."

But I couldn't finish this time, either, because just then Paula Pecorino and Rattington von Cheese Curd reached the pier.

They were **ARGUING LOUDLY**.

We needed to go right!

"I told you we needed to go right!" the rugby player **GROWLED**, waving her paw in the air.

"Right through that field of **thornbushes**? We never would have made it!"

"Are you saying that

it's my fault we didn't find the FLAG?!" Paula yelled.

"I'm not saying it's your fault," Rattington said. "I'm just saying that your RUDE behavior certainly didn't help!"

Smoothie got up from his chair. "Hey, no arguing allowed! It sounds like you just had a few setbacks."

Yikes. Trap and I exchanged a look. It sounded like their team had had more than a few setbacks. I opened my snout to share my news, but before I could say anything, Sally silenced everyone by whistling loudly.

"You've all lost! We won!" Then she grabbed Gal in a hug. "We did it, Gal! We'll get the scoop at Mouse Luxe resort!"

But she SQUEEZED her teammate so tightly that the mouselet's necklace broke off and fell to the ground.

CLANG!!!

Gal rushed to grab it, but just then the pendant started to talk!

Squeak?!

The recorded voice of a rodent boomed out: *"Listen, you will have an orienteering challenge. Smoothie will give you a map and a compass. I'll tell you how to sabotage the others . . ."*

Toasted cheese triangles!
What was going on?!

A Spy in the Competition

Sally and Gal had gone as pale as two slices of **provolone** cheese.

"There's a **device** hidden inside Gal's pendant that can receive messages!" I cried.

Trap shook his snout in disappointment. "Cell phones and other communication devices are against the rules. **You cheated!**"

Paula Pecorino stomped her paw. "You have to disqualify them!"

Everyone looked at Gal, who stood **SPEECHLESS**, staring down at her **BROKEN** necklace.

"Wait, I recognize that voice," Smoothie said. "That's the journalist from *The Rat Report* tabloid. Just yesterday I gave him an exclusive **interview**. I told him all the details of the final challenge."

Paula looked so angry that I was surprised not to see **FLAMES** shooting out of her

whiskers. "Well, it looks like that rat went right to Sally and blabbed about the whole thing!" she thundered.

"That stinky rat!" Smoothie muttered. "I trusted him!"

Rattington von Cheese Curd sighed. "This is all very **annoying**. Are there any good snacks for us?"

"Wait!" I cried. I wanted to know about the snacks, too, but something had just occurred to me. "I recognize that voice, too . . . That was the voice of Pawsley Pinhead, the managing editor of *The Daily Rat*! There is no tabloid called *The Rat Report* — he lied to you!"

I turned to Sally Ratmousen, who was innocently examining her **purple** painted nails.

I pointed to her and said, "Isn't that true?"

She gave me an icy glare. "I don't know what any of you are talking about. We won. Fair and cheese square."

Smoothie held up his paws. "Not so FAST now. This is all very confusing. I can't name you the winner until I understand what's going on!"

A tense silence fell over the sad beaches of Port Stinky.

Suddenly, Gal, looking DISTRESSED, spoke up. "You're right . . . Sally made me hide a messaging device in my necklace. She used it to communicate with Pawsley. That way he could help us with the challenges! First he sent us instructions on how to build the perfect hut. Then he interviewed

Pawsley Pinhead

Smoothie so that he could give us the details of the final challenge ahead of time!"

Sally, next to her, huffed and waved her paws as if shooing away invisible flies. Squeak, she seemed ready to explode!

Gal continued. "Sally made me go into the forest at **night** while everyone was sleeping to get rid of the other teams' second flags . . ."

Holey Swiss cheese, she hadn't been taking relaxing **nighttime** strolls — she'd been committing sabotage!

"That's why we couldn't FIND the second flag," Paula cried. "There wasn't one to find!"

Gal turned to Sally. "I'm sorry, but I couldn't keep *lying*. I was taught that a journalist must always tell the truth!"

Sally STAMPED her paw on the pier

with irritation. "I've heard enough! You're fired, you ungrateful slimy cheese! Starting tomorrow, you will no longer be a part of *The Daily Rat*! Your career is finished, I tell you!"

With that, she **STOMPED** off alone toward our huts, **FUMING**.

I watched her go, twisting my tail in my paws. That wasn't how I saw the competition going!

THE WINNERS!

Smoothie turned back to us. "Mice, now that the **PLOT** has been revealed, there's only one thing to do."

I held my **breath**. I hoped we wouldn't have to start the competition all over from the beginning. There was no way I was ever **jumping** out of a helicopter again!

"I'm very pleased to announce that we have two winning teams!" Smoothie continued. "Congratulations, Paula Pecorino and Rattington von Cheese Curd, AND Geronimo Stilton and his cousin Trap! Get ready for an **amaze-mouse** vacation at

the super-mega-resort, **Mouse Luxe**!"

With that, Smoothie turned his radio back on and started to dance.

"**Mouse Luxe**, here we come!" Trap cheered.

Paula let out an excited **whoop** and hugged Rattington. "I'm sorry I treated you so badly!" she said to Rattington.

"I'm sorry I was so cranky," he said.

I shed a little tear as I watched them make up. I have a heart as soft as mascarpone! My whiskers twitched with excitement. I couldn't wait to be sipping a cheese smoothie on a real beach. One that didn't smell.

That's when I remembered my news: THE GHOST ORCHID!

I ran to turn off Smoothie's radio.

"Hey, Geronimo, what gives?"

"We must return to New Mouse City immediately!" I cried.

Smoothie tried to object. "Why should we do that? The party is just starting! Why are you being such a stinky cheese?"

"We must return to New Mouse City immediately because I have made an INCREDIMOUSE discovery!"

At last, I had everyone's attention. I told them about the super-rare GHOST ORCHID that Trap and I had found in the forest.

"Why, that's wonderful!" Smoothie said. "That means this area is not as much of a lost cause as we all thought. With a little bit of help, I bet it could be rehabilitated even further!"

"We must get this news out," Gal said.

Even Smoothie agreed. "Let's go! This business with the orchid is a real fabumouse DISCOVERY. Just think, Port Stinky could have a second life as a nature tourism hot spot!"

His eyes sparkled at the thought.

Hmm . . . Did he only ever think of tourism? But I **shrugged**. We collected our belongings and got ready to board the helicopter. Sally emerged from her hut to join us for the ride home.

This had been some ADVENTURE. I couldn't wait to get home. Squeak!!

BIG NEWS AT *THE RODENT'S GAZETTE*!

At my office two days later, we had just gone to print with the **breaking** news about Port Stinky's ecological rebound. I couldn't wait for the entire island to learn about the GHOST ORCHID and what it meant for the once-abandoned area.

I was very nervous about what rodents would think!

I ran back and forth asking the staff questions.

"Did you reread the article like I asked? Were there any typos?"

"No typos!" replied the proofreader.

"And what about the website? Are we getting a lot of views?" I asked.

"We are!" our webmaster said. "And lots of positive comments already."

"And the photos? Do the photos look okay?" I asked.

"Yes, they look **FABUMOUSE**," said my sister, Thea, special correspondent for my newspaper, with a sigh. "Here, take another look at the images." She handed me her tablet so I could flip through the story on our website. I prefer the way it looks in print, but this is nice, too.

Geronimo Stilton

THE RODENT'S GAZETTE

A rare ghost orchid has been discovered in the heart of an area once deemed hopeless!

In spite of the terrible pollution that has affected the area of Port Stinky, today hope returns: in the heart of the forest, nature has been reborn!

"Nervous, Geronimo?" Trap asked, SURPRISING me. I nearly dropped Thea's tablet. "Such a shame that we had to postpone our luxury vacation while you worked on this story."

"I know that things didn't work out the way you were hoping, but this was really **important**. Thanks for being so understanding," I said.

"I'm sure that this will be a very successful issue!" Thea said. "We'll generate lots of support to clean up the beach and purify the water."

I nodded. "Some of the experts I talked to thought there will even be an opportunity to turn the old factory into a center for the observation and conservation of plants and animals! Port Stinky is like a real-time experiment in progress."

Trap sighed. "That all sounds great, but . . . a resort vacation would have been pretty nice, too . . ."

I watched the comments roll in on our Port Stinky article. All that hard work for the competition had paid off — just not in the way we thought it would!

In the months that followed, the transformation of **Port Stinky** kicked into high gear. When it was finally open to the general public, I had a **FABUMOUSE** idea . . .

One morning, I knocked on Trap's door. "I have a present for you!" I cried.

"What is it?" Trap said.

I pulled a flyer from my jacket POCKET. "It's a voucher from the Trust Me You'll Like It agency to finally take that vacation we won. But we're not going to Mouse Luxe!"

"We're not?" Trap asked, his snout falling.

"No! We're going someplace better," I said. "Port Stinky!!"

When we arrived for our mouse-luxurious stay, we found a totally transformed area.

The beaches had been cleaned of litter, the sea was a clear, bright **blue**, and the forest was healthy and thriving. Freshly cleared paths made it possible to take long walks through the **TREES**. Visitors were encouraged to follow guide mice on trips to admire the many species present . . . obviously including the enchanting GHOST ORCHID!

Above all, the air at last smelled sweet and clean.

Port Stinky would need a new name!

In the end, even Trap had to admit that this was better than anything we could have planned.

"Geronimo, I think that this vacation at Port Stinky is even better than going to the **Mouse Luxe** resort would have been."

I grinned. "Just think, if we hadn't gotten

chased by that skunk, none of this
would have happened!"

Trap burst out **laughing**, and I

joined in. Maybe **Port Stinky** was the perfect name for this place, after all!

Don't miss a single fabumouse adventure!

☐ #1 Lost Treasure of the Emerald Eye
☐ #2 The Curse of the Cheese Pyramid
☐ #3 Cat and Mouse in a Haunted House
☐ #4 I'm Too Fond of My Fur!
☐ #5 Four Mice Deep in the Jungle
☐ #6 Paws Off, Cheddarface!
☐ #7 Red Pizzas for a Blue Count
☐ #8 Attack of the Bandit Cats
☐ #9 A Fabumouse Vacation for Geronimo
☐ #10 All Because of a Cup of Coffee
☐ #11 It's Halloween, You 'Fraidy Mouse!
☐ #12 Merry Christmas, Geronimo!
☐ #13 The Phantom of the Subway
☐ #14 The Temple of the Ruby of Fire
☐ #15 The Mona Mousa Code

☐ #16 A Cheese-Colored Camper
☐ #17 Watch Your Whiskers, Stilton!
☐ #18 Shipwreck on the Pirate Islands
☐ #19 My Name Is Stilton, Geronimo Stilton
☐ #20 Surf's Up, Geronimo!
☐ #21 The Wild, Wild West
☐ #22 The Secret of Cacklefur Castle
☐ A Christmas Tale
☐ #23 Valentine's Day Disaster
☐ #24 Field Trip to Niagara Falls
☐ #25 The Search for Sunken Treasure
☐ #26 The Mummy with No Name
☐ #27 The Christmas Toy Factory
☐ #28 Wedding Crasher
☐ #29 Down and Out Down Under

☐ #30 The Mouse Island Marathon
☐ #31 The Mysterious Cheese Thief
☐ Christmas Catastrophe
☐ #32 Valley of the Giant Skeletons
☐ #33 Geronimo and the Gold Medal Mystery
☐ #34 Geronimo Stilton, Secret Agent
☐ #35 A Very Merry Christmas
☐ #36 Geronimo's Valentine
☐ #37 The Race Across America
☐ #38 A Fabumouse School Adventure
☐ #39 Singing Sensation
☐ #40 The Karate Mouse
☐ #41 Mighty Mount Kilimanjaro
☐ #42 The Peculiar Pumpkin Thief
☐ #43 I'm Not a Supermouse!
☐ #44 The Giant Diamond Robbery
☐ #45 Save the White Whale!
☐ #46 The Haunted Castle
☐ #47 Run for the Hills, Geronimo!
☐ #48 The Mystery in Venice
☐ #49 The Way of the Samurai
☐ #50 This Hotel Is Haunted!
☐ #51 The Enormouse Pearl Heist
☐ #52 Mouse in Space!
☐ #53 Rumble in the Jungle
☐ #54 Get into Gear, Stilton!
☐ #55 The Golden Statue Plot
☐ #56 Flight of the Red Bandit
☐ #57 The Stinky Cheese Vacation
☐ #58 The Super Chef Contest

☐ #59 Welcome to Moldy Manor
☐ #60 The Treasure of Easter Island
☐ #61 Mouse House Hunter
☐ #62 Mouse Overboard!
☐ #63 The Cheese Experiment
☐ #64 Magical Mission
☐ #65 Bollywood Burglary
☐ #66 Operation: Secret Recipe
☐ #67 The Chocolate Chase
☐ #68 Cyber-Thief Showdown
☐ #69 Hug a Tree, Geronimo
☐ #70 The Phantom Bandit
☐ #71 Geronimo on Ice!
☐ #72 The Hawaiian Heist
☐ #73 The Missing Movie
☐ #74 Happy Birthday, Geronimo!
☐ #75 The Sticky Situation
☐ #76 Superstore Surprise
☐ #77 The Last Resort Oasis
☐ #78 Mysterious Eye of the Dragon
☐ #79 Garbage Dump Disaster
☐ #80 Have a Heart, Geronimo
☐ #81 The Super Cup Face-Off
☐ #82 Mouse VS Wild

You've never seen Geronimo Stilton like this before!

Get your paws on the all-new

Geronimo Stilton

graphic novels. You've gouda* have them!

Don't miss any of my adventures in the Kingdom of Fantasy!

THE KINGDOM OF FANTASY

THE QUEST FOR PARADISE:
THE RETURN TO THE KINGDOM OF FANTASY

THE AMAZING VOYAGE:
THE THIRD ADVENTURE IN THE KINGDOM OF FANTASY

THE DRAGON PROPHECY:
THE FOURTH ADVENTURE IN THE KINGDOM OF FANTASY

THE VOLCANO OF FIRE:
THE FIFTH ADVENTURE IN THE KINGDOM OF FANTASY

THE SEARCH FOR TREASURE:
THE SIXTH ADVENTURE IN THE KINGDOM OF FANTASY

THE ENCHANTED CHARMS:
THE SEVENTH ADVENTURE IN THE KINGDOM OF FANTASY

THE PHOENIX OF DESTINY:
AN EPIC KINGDOM OF FANTASY ADVENTURE

THE HOUR OF MAGIC:
THE EIGHTH ADVENTURE IN THE KINGDOM OF FANTASY

THE WIZARD'S WAND:
THE NINTH ADVENTURE IN THE KINGDOM OF FANTASY

THE SHIP OF SECRETS:
THE TENTH ADVENTURE IN THE KINGDOM OF FANTASY

THE DRAGON OF FORTUNE:
AN EPIC KINGDOM OF FANTASY ADVENTURE

THE GUARDIAN OF THE REALM:
THE ELEVENTH ADVENTURE IN THE KINGDOM OF FANTASY

THE ISLAND OF DRAGONS:
THE TWELFTH ADVENTURE IN THE KINGDOM OF FANTASY

THE BATTLE FOR THE CRYSTAL CASTLE:
THE THIRTEENTH ADVENTURE IN THE KINGDOM OF FANTASY

THE KEEPERS OF THE EMPIRE:
THE FOURTEENTH ADVENTURE IN THE KINGDOM OF FANTASY

THE GOLDEN KEY
THE FIFTEENTH ADVENTURE IN THE KINGDOM OF FANTASY

Thea Stilton

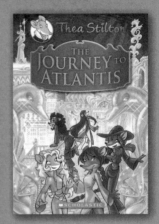

Special Editions

Don't miss any of these exciting series featuring the Thea Sisters!

Treasure Seekers

Mouseford Academy

Don't miss any of my fabumouse special editions!

THE JOURNEY
TO ATLANTIS

THE SECRET OF
THE FAIRIES

THE SECRET OF
THE SNOW

THE CLOUD
CASTLE

THE TREASURE
OF THE SEA

THE LAND OF
FLOWERS

THE SECRET OF
THE CRYSTAL
FAIRIES

THE DANCE OF
THE STAR FAIRIES

THE MAGIC OF
THE MIRROR

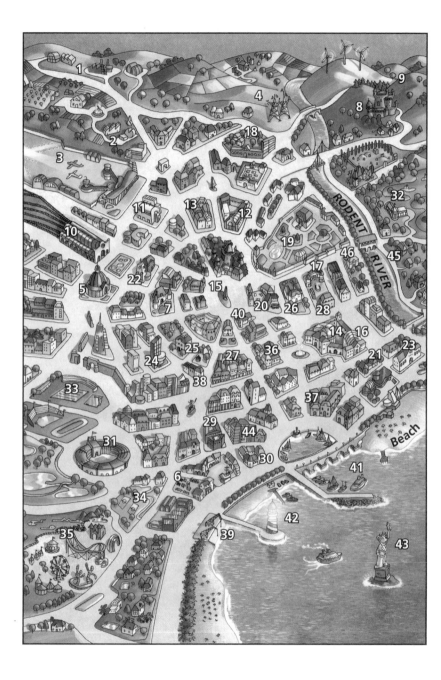

Map of New Mouse City

1. Industrial Zone
2. Cheese Factories
3. Angorat International Airport
4. WRAT Radio and Television Station
5. Cheese Market
6. Fish Market
7. Town Hall
8. Snotnose Castle
9. The Seven Hills of Mouse Island
10. Mouse Central Station
11. Trade Center
12. Movie Theater
13. Gym
14. Catnegie Hall
15. Singing Stone Plaza
16. The Gouda Theater
17. Grand Hotel
18. Mouse General Hospital
19. Botanical Gardens
20. Cheap Junk for Less (Trap's store)
21. Aunt Sweetfur and Benjamin's House
22. Mouseum of Modern Art
23. University and Library
24. *The Daily Rat*
25. *The Rodent's Gazette*
26. Trap's House
27. Fashion District
28. The Mouse House Restaurant
29. Environmental Protection Center
30. Harbor Office
31. Mousidon Square Garden
32. Golf Course
33. Swimming Pool
34. Tennis Courts
35. Curlyfur Island Amusement Park
36. Geronimo's House
37. Historic District
38. Public Library
39. Shipyard
40. Thea's House
41. New Mouse Harbor
42. Luna Lighthouse
43. The Statue of Liberty
44. Hercule Poirat's Office
45. Petunia Pretty Paws's House
46. Grandfather William's House

Brigand's Isle

This way to the Rodent Straits

Tomcat Island

Pirate Ship of Cats

2
3
4

1

Cat's Claw Bay

Panther Archipelago

Hamster Islands

Blue Dolphin Bay

6
7

5

Swissville

Coral Reefs

This way to the Mousific Ocean

Stray Cat Harbor

25

8

9

14

11
13

12

Cheddarton

10

23

Mouseport

32

15

21

22

This way to the Ratlantic Ocean

San Mouscisco

20

29
19
18

26

17
16

New Mouse City

35

24

Mousefort Beach

28

30

27

31
36

33

37

34

Furflung Island

N
W   E
S

MOUSE ISLAND

This way to the Sea of Mice

Map of Mouse Island

<table>
<tr><td>1.</td><td>Big Ice Lake</td><td>21.</td><td>Lake Lakelake</td></tr>
<tr><td>2.</td><td>Frozen Fur Peak</td><td>22.</td><td>Lake Lakelakelake</td></tr>
<tr><td>3.</td><td>Slipperyslopes Glacier</td><td>23.</td><td>Cheddar Crag</td></tr>
<tr><td>4.</td><td>Coldcreeps Peak</td><td>24.</td><td>Cannycat Castle</td></tr>
<tr><td>5.</td><td>Ratzikistan</td><td>25.</td><td>Valley of the Giant</td></tr>
<tr><td>6.</td><td>Transratania</td><td></td><td>Sequoia</td></tr>
<tr><td>7.</td><td>Mount Vamp</td><td>26.</td><td>Cheddar Springs</td></tr>
<tr><td>8.</td><td>Roastedrat Volcano</td><td>27.</td><td>Sulfurous Swamp</td></tr>
<tr><td>9.</td><td>Brimstone Lake</td><td>28.</td><td>Old Reliable Geyser</td></tr>
<tr><td>10.</td><td>Poopedcat Pass</td><td>29.</td><td>Vole Vale</td></tr>
<tr><td>11.</td><td>Stinko Peak</td><td>30.</td><td>Ravingrat Ravine</td></tr>
<tr><td>12.</td><td>Dark Forest</td><td>31.</td><td>Gnat Marshes</td></tr>
<tr><td>13.</td><td>Vain Vampires Valley</td><td>32.</td><td>Munster Highlands</td></tr>
<tr><td>14.</td><td>Goose Bumps Gorge</td><td>33.</td><td>Mousehara Desert</td></tr>
<tr><td>15.</td><td>The Shadow Line Pass</td><td>34.</td><td>Oasis of the</td></tr>
<tr><td>16.</td><td>Penny Pincher Castle</td><td></td><td>Sweaty Camel</td></tr>
<tr><td>17.</td><td>Nature Reserve Park</td><td>35.</td><td>Cabbagehead Hill</td></tr>
<tr><td>18.</td><td>Las Ratayas Marinas</td><td>36.</td><td>Rattytrap Jungle</td></tr>
<tr><td>19.</td><td>Fossil Forest</td><td>37.</td><td>Rio Mosquito</td></tr>
<tr><td>20.</td><td>Lake Lake</td><td></td><td></td></tr>
</table>

Dear mouse friends,
Thanks for reading, and farewell
till the next book.
It'll be another whisker-licking-good
adventure, and that's a promise!

Geronimo Stilton